Turtle on a Summer's Day

Turtle

on a

Summer's Day

ᘓ

Written by Frances Gilbert
Illustrated by Sarah Frances

For Grandad
who would have read this to Matthew

It was a hot, sticky summer afternoon.

Turtle was bored.

"Play with me, Father," he said. But Father said, "I am busy, run along, and put on your sandals."

"Play with me Mother," he said. But Mother said, "I am busy, run along, and put on your sun hat."

So Turtle put on his sandals and his sun hat and went outside.

He was going to ask Baby to play with him, but Mother called out, "Don't wake Baby!"

Turtle sat on the back doorstep in the sun and felt hot and crosser than ever in his sandals, his sun hat and his hot, thick shell.

"There's nothing to do," he said.

Down in the drowsy summer garden, Cat rolled and wriggled in the lavender. Then she s-t-r-e-t-c-h-e-d herself comfy along the wall.

She blinked her eyes and looked at Turtle.

In the dapple-light under the trees, Bird fluttered and spluttered in his puddle-bath. Then he shook himself off and rested airy on a branch.

He tipped his head and watched Turtle.

Along the sunny gravel path came Snake, slithering and twisting. She coiled herself around the watering can, under the trickle of cool water.

She flicked her tongue and gazed at Turtle.

Beneath the thorny bushes, Dog yawned and dug himself a dusty bed. He fitted into it to doze in the shade.

But now and then he pricked his ears up at Turtle.

"My!" said Turtle. "I wish I could have fun like that." He looked to see if anybody was around to play with him. But Mother and Father were still busy and Baby was still sleeping.

"Well," said Turtle, "I will play like all my friends."

So naughty Turtle took off his sandals, took off his sun hat, and took off his shell. He danced down into the shady summer garden, free and light in his little bare skin.

Then he played all afternoon and had a glorious time!

He rolled in the lavender. He s–t–r–e–t–c–h–e–d out along the wall and took a sun bath with Cat.

He splashed and spluttered in Bird's bath until he was soaked and wrinkled.

He practiced wriggling and slithering along Snake's sunny gravel path.

He scratched under the thorn bushes where Dog slept.

By and by, Turtle began to feel very poorly.

He was itchy and scratchy from the lavender. He was baked from the sun bath and scraped from the slithering. He was sore and sneezy from the dusty digging. His head ached and his tummy didn't feel at all right.

"I had better go home," he said.

"Well!" said Mother, "weren't you silly!" She put him under a cool shower and rinsed off the itchy bits of lavender. She stood him on the bathroom chair and dabbed his poor scratched, burnt itchy-skin self with cool, pink calamine. She gave him a big spoonful of medicine for his tummy.

Last of all, she dusted him with baby's powder and slipped him back into his shell. It felt just fine.

"Well," said Father when he came to read a bedtime story. "Did you have a good time playing in the garden?"

"No," said Turtle. "Cat and Bird and Snake and Dog had fun, but it was all wrong for me."

"What can you do about that?" said Father.

"Tomorrow, I will play in my sandpit," said Turtle, "but I'll keep my sandals, my sun hat and my shell on because I don't have any fur like Cat and Dog, or feathers like Bird, or a tummy for slithering like Snake."

"That's right," said Father, "you have to do what's right for you."

"I know," said Turtle, as he closed his eyes.